Praise for Storyshares

"One of the brightest innovators and game-changers in the education industry."
— Forbes

"Your success in applying research-validated practices to promote literacy serves as a valuable model for other organizations seeking to create evidence-based literacy programs."   — Library of Congress

"We need powerful social and educational innovation, and Storyshares is break-ing new ground. The organization addresses critical problems facing our stu-dents and teachers. I am excited about the strategies it brings to the collective work of making sure every student has an equal chance in life."
— Teach For America

"It's the perfect idea. There's really nothing like this. I mean, wow, this will be a wonderful experience for young people."   — Andrea Davis Pinkney, Executive Director, Scholastic

"Reading for meaning opens opportunities for a lifetime of learning. Providing emerging readers with engaging texts that are designed to offer both challenges and support for each individual will improve their lives for years to come. Story-shares is a wonderful start."   — David Rose, Co-founder of CAST & UD_

Whispers of the Unknown

Storyshares presents

ISBN 9798885976794

Storyshares
Storyshares, LLC
24 N. Bryn Mawr Avenue #340
Bryn Mawr, PA 19010-3304
www.storyshares.org

Inspiring reading with a new kind of book.

Fortune Teller copyright 2024 Dylan Schatell
Interest Level: Post High School   **Grade Level Equivalent:** 3.5

The Double copyright 2024 Emma Chambers
Interest Level: Post High School   **Grade Level Equivalent:** 4.5

The Henry Woman copyright 2024 Dinko Dinev
Interest Level: Post High School   **Grade Level Equivalent:** 3.7

Book design by Saskia Globig

WHISPERS OF THE UNKNOWN

a collection of haunting stories

Storyshares

CONTENTS

FORTUNE TELLER

Dylan Schatell

CHAPTER ONE

"I guess this could be fun," said Oliver.

The three friends stood outside a small, old, beaten building. They were wandering around the historic district in downtown Salem, Massachusetts.

None of them had med school classes that day, so they decided to visit Salem and tour the city. Since it was October, they thought visiting Salem and seeing all the Halloween decorations would be fun.

"Ok, so I know it's not real, guys, but I thought it might be fun, you know? It might get us into the Halloween mood," said Ben.

Orange and red leaves covered the ground,

leaving the trees barren. It was cold. Cool fall air blew on Ben's neck. He wore just shorts and a t-shirt while Annie and Oliver wore sweaters.

"How are you not freezing right now?" asked Oliver.

"I don't know. How are you not hot right now?" asked Ben.

The old building in front of them looked beaten down, and its wooden front peeled. It was a part of a decent-sized group of small shops. This store stood at the very end of the group. The glass showed several small objects that looked like they would sell at a pawn shop for a few bucks.

The sign read Mr. Proctor's Magic Shop. It was also worn down. One of the Os had fallen off and an R was missing. One could still make out what it said due to the remaining outline of the missing letters. Another sign hanging down said OPEN.

"Let's go in, but I don't really wanna get my fortune told," said Annie. "I don't wanna give my money to some fake who plays with people's feelings."

CHAPTER TWO

Ben, Annie, and Oliver stepped into the store. At once, they smelled the musty air. The whole store felt old. No one was at the front desk, so they decided to check out the products until the owner or whoever worked there showed up.

"I gotta say, Ben, you were right about Salem," said Oliver. "They really do go all out for Halloween."

"This place looks so old that I think it could've been here during the actual Salem witch trials," said Annie.

"Damn, some of this stuff is pretty creepy. I bet this guy tries to make the most money he can over the spooky season," said Oliver.

He picked up a book from the shelf. It was covered in dust, which he quickly blew off.

"This book says *Practical Kabbalah*. It has a bunch of Hebrew on it. I think it's some kind of book about Jewish magic." He held it up for Ben and Annie to see and then put it back down. "I definitely don't remember learning about this stuff in Hebrew school," he laughed.

As Ben walked around the store, he looked at the figurines. Some were pretty antique-looking. They looked like they might break the second he touched them.

"How do these things last so long without breaking?" he whispered to himself.

He walked around a little more until he saw a figure that caught his eye. A man sat playing the violin, wearing clothing from three or four hundred years ago. The face was as white as the wig above it.

What really made Ben interested were its eyes. Ben had always heard how people said that the Mona Lisa's eyes looked like they followed you, but he could never see it.

This figurine, however... Ben could've sworn that its eyes were following him. And not just following, but deeper. Almost like something was behind those eyes. Watching him.

Ben looked around the room at all the other figurines. He noticed they all had the same effect. No matter where he stood in the room, it looked like each one was staring at him. Like he was an intruder in a play.

CHAPTER THREE

"Hello! I'll be with you in just a second!" yelled a man from the back room. He had what Ben thought was an English accent, but not one he had ever really heard before. It sounded like a mix between an English and Southern accent.

Annie, Oliver, and Ben walked up to the front desk. Behind it sat an older man, probably in his late fifties or sixties. He had light gray hair kept somewhat short, along with a gray mustache and goatee. His eyes were glassy and cloudy. He had a wide grin and perfect, shiny, white teeth.

His most notable feature was a mark going around his neck. It looked like he had been cut there or something. Ben thought it best not to stare. Although with the man being blind, he probably wouldn't even notice.

"What can I do for you today?" asked the older man.

"We heard you do tarot card readings?" asked Ben. "I wanted to see if you could do one for me."

"Why, of course! That will be thirty-five dollars."

"Sure, I'll pay that."

"All right. Let me get my cards from the back. It may take me a bit to find them, so why don't you all look around? Maybe something might catch your eye."

CHAPTER FOUR

Ben, Oliver, and Annie began to wander the store again. Oliver picked up a book titled *Magick In Theory and Practice* by Aleister Crowley.

"You're really gonna waste thirty-five dollars on this?" asked Oliver. He opened the book and skimmed through it.

"It's not really a waste, though. It might be fun," Ben said.

"I agree with Ben," said Annie.

She stood a few feet away, looking in a box. Inside were a bunch of mason jars, all seemingly empty. She picked one up and saw that it had a piece of tape on it with the name Abigail Williams written in script.

Ben walked back over to the violinist figurine from earlier. He noticed that this time, the eyes didn't look like they were following him. Rather, they looked like they were staring at Annie in the corner. Ben moved his face closer to the figurine to get a better look.

As he leaned closer, he suddenly felt a cold chill. His neck felt wet, like water droplets were falling on it. He backed up and felt the back of his neck with his hand, but felt no water.

"All right, come back. I found them," said the older man. He started shuffling the deck around. "Now, what's your name, lad?"

"Ben."

"I'm Mr. Proctor," he said. "Let's begin the tarot reading."

CHAPTER FIVE

Mr. Proctor shuffled the deck. He drew the first card, not even lowering his head toward it. He simply felt it and knew what it was, probably because he had done it so many times before.

The table had a purple mat with magical-looking marks on it. A couple of items lay on it: an empty jar with the lid removed, a glass frog figure, and a jar filled with some brown liquid.

Mr. Proctor set down the first card and said, "The Reversed Devil."

The card was upside down and had a picture of the Devil and two people next to him on it. The card looked straight out of the early nineteenth century, yet had no visible signs of wear and tear.

"This first card represents your past. A Reversed Devil means that you feel trapped."

Ben thought for a second. "I do feel trapped. I want to quit med school, but at the same time, I don't want to disappoint my family."

Oliver spoke up. "Yeah, maybe, but everyone feels trapped sometimes."

Mr. Proctor glared at him and then went back to facing Ben. "The next card I draw will show your present or near future."

This card had a picture of a blindfolded woman holding two crossed swords.

"The Upright Two of Swords. This card means that you will make a very important decision in your very near future. One that will have a serious impact on your life."

"I assume this means I will choose to either leave or stay in med school in the very near future." Ben closed his eyes. "That pretty much would have to be it. I can't think of any other big decisions I would make."

Mr. Proctor grinned for a moment. "That probably is it, wouldn't you say?" He picked up the next card and put it on the table face down.

"This card represents your future. It will be the final card I draw."

He flipped it over. The card showed a tower being destroyed with fire and two people jumping out of it.

"The Tower. This card represents crisis and ruin."

CHAPTER SIX

Ben looked up at Mr. Proctor.

"What would that mean for me?"

"It means that the result of your decision will end very badly for you."

"That's definitely not good," laughed Ben.

Mr. Proctor gave a short laugh as well. "Well, that'll be thirty-five dollars."

He held out his hand. Ben pulled out his wallet and gave Mr. Proctor the money.

"Feel free to look around the rest of my store," Mr. Proctor said. "I'll be in the back if you need anything."

Ben, Oliver, and Annie started wandering the

store again and looking at the objects.

"That was a complete waste of time and money, right? We can all agree on that?" asked Oliver.

"It was a little fun," said Annie.

"I agree. You know what? Maybe he did provide me with a little understanding," Ben said.

Oliver looked at him in shock. "You're not telling me you actually believe in this stuff?"

"No, but I mean... Maybe there's some credit to it. So many people believe in it, and millions of people can't be entirely wrong, can they?"

"They absolutely can," said Oliver.

"I'm a little worried now. He said that my decision will end badly for me. Maybe that's not true, but honestly I think it might be," Ben said.

Annie spoke up. "Well, let's assume for a second his guess is true.

"You still don't know which option will bring you negative consequences. So maybe it can be avoided if you choose correctly.

"You just have to figure out which choice that is."

CHAPTER SEVEN

"I don't think so," Ben said. "If his guess is true, then no matter what I choose, it will have bad effects. I can't avoid the future. But let's go back to thinking it's all just a load of crap.

"If I leave med school, I disappoint my family and possibly get cut off. And then what? I want to be a musician, but I probably won't make much money. I've never even supported myself before. My parents always did, and—"

"Calm down for a minute," said Oliver. "What if you don't quit med school?"

"I'd probably be very unhappy because I don't want to be a doctor."

"I mean, you could just try to keep making music as a hobby. If you truly love music, then it should be about the creation, not the fame. So keeping it as a hobby would work out," said Oliver.

"Maybe you should do what you love," said Annie. "If you really think you'll be unhappy, then shouldn't your own joy outweigh what your parents want? I mean, my father would've loved it if I had competed in chess like him, but I chose to go to med school because helping people is what I love to do."

"It's not the same, though," Ben said, "because chess wouldn't be a full-time career. Being a musician would." He now looked a little uneasy.

"I mean you are great at chess, but I don't know if people would like my music. If I became a full-time musician and people didn't like my songs, then what? I'd be alone and broke. Honestly, I think the bad decision that I make will be becoming a musician."

Mr. Proctor spoke up from behind the counter. "You know, I might be able to help with that."

CHAPTER EIGHT

Annie, Ben, and Oliver turned around and looked at Mr. Proctor.

"How so?" asked Ben.

"I know quite a few secret tricks. For a price, of course, I could possibly help you become not only a great musician, but a beloved one. The greatest in the world, for the rest of your life."

"OK, now we know for sure he's full of crap," said Oliver. "Let's go, guys. He's messing with you, Ben."

Ben looked at the old man's face. He could feel something sneaky in him. But Ben heard something whisper in his ear—or maybe he only felt like something did. He knew he was being told to go to the old man.

"How could you do that?"

"It's rather simple. I know a spell I could use to give you more musical talent than anyone you can think of."

"I swear, you're so easy to trick if you actually listen to him. I'm waiting outside," said an annoyed Oliver.

He walked out. Annie followed.

Ben felt the room's temperature drop. It became colder by the second.

He looked around and saw the antiques around the shop. Again, they looked like they were staring at him.

Ben looked Mr. Proctor in his cloudy eyes. He knew Mr. Proctor was blind, but he couldn't shake the feeling that Mr. Proctor knew he was staring.

"What will it be?" Mr. Proctor asked. "Shake my hand, and the deal is done."

"How much will it cost?" Ben asked.

"Nothing more than what you already have on your person." The old man stuck out his hand. His palms were dry and peeling. Ben took his hand and felt its cold grip.

"When do you think that awful decision I make will actually happen?" asked Ben.

He felt the old man's cold grip heat up.

Ben's right arm started to feel weak and heavy. It was shrinking. Ben looked back up at the younger man standing in front of him.

"It already has."

THE DOUBLE

Emma Chambers

CHAPTER ONE

On the seventh of July 1996, Camilla ran away from her life and never went back.

She quit her job at the cafe and booked a one-way train ticket. She was armed with nothing but a dusty red suitcase, her typewriter, and Henry, who was sulking in a cat carrier.

She had left a note on the kitchen counter for Maria to find when she got back from her business trip.

Other than that, she had said no goodbyes.

Fortunately, her grandmother had a cottage in the English countryside.

She could stay for as long as she liked.

It was the perfect place to write her novel in peace.

CHAPTER TWO

She hadn't been to the cottage since her mother died. She was ready for it to be cluttered and dusty, having been abandoned for so long.

Ever since she was 17 or 18, time had felt less like a friend and more like an enemy that she was never able to outrun.

The disorder of the cottage reminded her just how long her mother had been dead. It also reminded her that violence could take many forms.

No force other than the relentless passage of time had caused the quiet destruction that greeted her in the countryside.

CHAPTER THREE

Camilla spent the first few days cleaning and repairing the cottage. She'd found a small selection of cleaning supplies. They had been tucked away in the shed behind the cottage years ago.

But that was all.

She didn't have time to paint, sand, or polish. It meant that furniture stayed in bad condition.

Except for one piece.

The one piece of furniture that was miraculously well kept was her grandmother's writing desk.

Its dark mahogany surface was shiny and smooth as ever.

As if only days had gone by, not years.

CHAPTER FOUR

She walked an hour or so to the nearest town. She bought six bags of groceries.

She bribed the store clerk to let her keep the grocery cart. She used it to get all her groceries back to the cottage.

Finally, everything was in order, and she was ready to write. She had 300 index cards, four empty notebooks and two full ones, and her old typewriter.

It was time to begin.

CHAPTER FIVE

She could feel the heartbeat of her novel inside of her. Ready to come to life.

She had begun working on this story about a month before.

Soon, it felt more important than anything. More important than any and all distractions.

So important, she knew she had to disappear from the world in order to bring her novel to life.

CHAPTER SIX

Many writers and artists alike experienced moments of great passion. Just as she was experiencing now.

It drove many of them insane.

Their writing had been brilliant, though. Even if they had died too young at the bottom of a lake or a bottle.

Camilla was certain she wouldn't suffer such a fate. She would survive this moment of great passion and creativity.

After all, she had gotten used to her moments of insanity.

She was able to control them, without help from a doctor or a pill.

CHAPTER SEVEN

Camilla had named the main character of her story Anna.

She'd chosen that name because she liked that it was spelled the same way backward and forward.

It was a mirror of itself.

As many writers do, Camilla had based Anna somewhat on herself.

She had learned that writers could be brilliant and have mood swings. But she'd also learned writers were often self-absorbed.

Creative people often confused self-awareness with self-obsession.

Camilla suspected she might be one of those creative people. She just didn't care enough to really figure it out.

CHAPTER EIGHT

Anna, she found, was a deeply flawed character.

She preferred beauty over everything else. Even if it meant denying anything ugly.

This made Anna an unhappy character when the ugly reality of life caught up with her.

She would have to leave her beautiful bubble and face reality. Camilla decided against creating an outline of her novel.

She never did with any book. There was no reason for this one to be different.

She started by writing the last chapter.

This way, she would have at least a faint idea of where the story was going.

Like putting a destination on an otherwise blank map.

CHAPTER NINE

She wrote it first in one of her blank note-books—a leatherbound one that Maria had given her for Christmas—and then typed it out on her typewriter and set it aside.

The ending was what she had figured out first. In fact, it was how she got the idea for the story.

That was something Camilla adored about writing: stories had endings.

Too often, she felt her own life needed the satisfaction of a real ending. An undeniable "the end."

Instead, one tragedy or success bled into another.

She was almost always robbed of a sense of finality.

CHAPTER TEN

This was probably also why she had a strange fascination with exit signs.

Wherever she was, she looked for them. If they were neon red or green, they seemed helpful and hopeful.

Once, after she and Maria had smoked three joints between them, they snuck into a public park well after midnight and stole one.

When they got home, they hung it above their door.

Camilla considered taking it with her to the cottage, but she didn't want Maria to feel trapped with it gone.

CHAPTER ELEVEN

Camilla lost her sense of time surprisingly quickly. She didn't wear a watch. There were no clocks in the cottage.

Only the sun could give her any indication of the time of day.

But she didn't really need to know the time, because she no longer had to live by it.

She slept when she was tired. She ate when she was hungry. In between, she wrote or she read, or she went on quiet walks in the woods surrounding her.

She spent hours at the old writing desk, typing with steady fury until her fingers ached.

That's when she was forced to take a cigarette break.

She made coffee in a French press whenever she felt like it. She ended up having to make a special trip into town just for coffee and milk.

CHAPTER TWELVE

The more she wrote, the more she fell in love with Anna.

She hadn't really outlined her character before she started writing. Camilla figured that Anna's character would reveal itself as the story progressed.

And anyway, Anna was supposed to be hard to understand, even to her own creator.

So Anna began to grow into a person as real as anyone who walked the earth. A person of flesh and bone, captured in words on a page.

How many of us are just the same? Camilla thought. Nothing more or less than ink on paper.

CHAPTER THIRTEEN

Sometimes when she was reading, sitting on the couch in the living room, she swore she could feel the weight of the couch shift.

It was like another person—Anna, undoubtedly—was sitting beside her.

She could all but see Anna looking over her shoulder with a dark red smile and sharp, piercing eyes.

Camilla wondered if the loneliness of the cottage was starting to affect her.

Only she didn't feel lonely; she simply felt alone.

She didn't mind being alone. Henry wasn't much for company. But she had found a strange comfort in Anna.

Anna had become a ghost of the cottage with whom Camilla could share anything, and be anyone. Even herself.

CHAPTER FOURTEEN

Anna rarely left her side. At first, Camilla was a little nervous about the situation.

She knew, of course, that Anna was not real.

Maybe she was a figment of Camilla's imagination. Maybe she was a vivid hallucination.

But soon, Anna had become a normal part of her life, like the couch itself. A comfort, yes, but a subtle and familiar one.

It was only when winter had descended like a swift fist that Camilla began to get scared.

CHAPTER FIFTEEN

There was only one mirror in the cottage. It was blurry with age and had a few cracks down the middle.

One night just as autumn turned into winter, Camilla passed the mirror.

In place of her own reflection was Anna's.

Anna's black hair and pale face made her blood red lips look even brighter.

Her eyes were barely open, like she was falling asleep. Her arms hung limply at her sides.

When Camilla took a careful step forward, the reflection didn't change.

Camilla chalked the incident up to the fact that she had slept very badly every night for almost two weeks. She went to sleep immediately after looking in the mirror.

She tried to avoid her reflection after that.

CHAPTER SIXTEEN

It didn't matter. Every time she caught even the slightest glimpse of herself, in the river or the silver gleam of a pot or pan, she always saw Anna's reflection.

Not hers.

Camilla ignored this. She decided it was because she was so connected to her character. So connected, her brain was making her think she was seeing Anna.

Surely it could only make her writing better.

CHAPTER SEVENTEEN

After a few weeks, Camilla realized that she couldn't quite remember what she looked like.

She would swear she had brown eyes... didn't she?

Her eyes were green, weren't they? It was Maria's that were brown.

She couldn't recall the shape of her face, or the way she looked when she smiled.

She tried and tried to get her reflection back.

After all, she had created Anna's reflection. She could get rid of it. But no matter what she did, whenever she looked, she saw Anna. Her perfect face. Her tired expression. Her strong posture.

All of it exactly the same.

CHAPTER EIGHTEEN

She had been so distracted with the loss of her reflection that she hadn't noticed Henry was missing.

She realized she hadn't seen him in a while. She couldn't say how long, though. His food bowl was full to the brim.

She knew it was irrational, but a small part of her was convinced that Anna had stolen him. Taken him into the mirror, where she was hiding.

She walked around the woods for hours one day, calling for Henry.

But he was gone.

CHAPTER NINETEEN

Another month or two went by, and she had for-gotten her own name.

She hadn't written it down anywhere.

Even if she had, she wouldn't know where to look for it.

In a fit of rage, she tore the mirror off the wall and threw it into the river. It vanished from sight.

She could finally be free of Anna.

But she wasn't free.

CHAPTER TWENTY

She still wandered around the cottage in a daze. It was like she was drugged.

She couldn't even put two thoughts together.

She hadn't spoken for so long that her voice had faded away entirely.

One afternoon, she became so overwhelmed that she let out a scream. It came from deep in her gut.

She felt it rise up from her toes.

Only nothing came out of her mouth.

Nothing but spit and air and rage so real she could almost see it.

CHAPTER TWENTY-ONE

The woman never left that cottage. Neither did Anna.

If you were to go there, you would find the place run down and almost collapsed.

You would find an almost complete manuscript with some of the most beautiful writing you would ever read.

Sitting there. Untouched, on an antique writing desk.

You would find Henry, who came back after some time, sleeping peacefully on the porch.

And you would find the body of one woman with two souls inside, trapped forever.

THE HENRY WOMAN

Dinko Dinev

CHAPTER ONE

Everything happened on a peaceful November night, nearly one year ago. I had just given the manuscript of my last novel to my literary agent. He's the guy who sells my books to publishing houses so *they* can sell my books.

He also gave me the check for my previous book. The money for this book was actually good, too.

One more check like that and I would finally be able to turn in my rusty Toyota Camry. I wanted something that would use less fuel and ride more comfortably.

Besides that, the money was enough for me to do nothing but write for the next two or three months. That would be enough time to finish the novel that was swirling in my head.

Now I'm a bit slower, but I am used to that.

Driving back home, I was thinking about the five-digit number on the check in my wallet. I smiled and said to myself, "You did it, Frank! You did it! You deserved that! No more doubts, no more anxious thoughts!"

The thing I had most wanted for the last two years had finally come true. I wasn't *just* a writer. I was a *successful* writer.

And even though I wasn't much of a drinker, I decided to celebrate my success with a shot or two in some local bar.

CHAPTER TWO

The traffic lights at 17th and Washington turned red.
I slowed down and stuck the tires right before the
white line.

There were no other cars on the road. I waited
anyway, smoking my last cigarette.

I took a long, final drag. Then I squeezed the
butt with two fingers and stuck it into the ashtray

The car had filled with smoke. I rolled the window down. The gray, bitter mist quickly began to
disappear.

I shifted to first gear, waiting for the red light to
turn green. A blue, shimmering light coming from
my right caught my eye.

The light came from the sign of a local bar

called Ronnie's. Half of the letters looked a bit dull and shady.

The bar was known as the place where nobody goes. I, personally, had never been there before. But on that night, something drew me like a giant magnet in its direction.

Without even knowing how, I had already turned right and was driving towards the bar. Even if it *were* empty, it would be comfortable to me.

Being—or drinking—on my own had never bothered me at all.

CHAPTER THREE

There was a convenience store right across from
the bar. I parked there and bought a pack of Camel
cigarettes. I crossed the street and entered
the bar.

Ronnie's.

Surprisingly, it wasn't as empty as I thought it
would be.

In the back, there were a bunch of people wearing leather jackets. Their arms were covered in
tattoos. They laughed loudly, banging on the wood-
en table.

At the bar were a couple of old, skinny men.
They were probably in their seventies. And they
were drinking in silence.

The air inside felt heavy and musty. The music was flat and sad, and the light was poor. I decided to stay.

I sat at the bar next to one of the old fellas. A young girl waited for my order. She was no more than twenty-one. Her brown hair fell just beneath her shoulders.

"Jack Daniel's, please. With no ice, please."

The girl poured the smooth, golden-brown liquid into a square glass and placed it in front of me.

"So, this is the 'place where nobody goes,' huh?" I asked.

The girl barely smiled and said nothing.

"Well, maybe you should change it to the 'place where somebody goes,'" I said and laughed lightly.

I drained the glass in one huge swallow. "One more, please."

CHAPTER FOUR

I opened up the pack of cigarettes and took one out. I lit it carefully and took a slow, deep drag. There was an ashtray. I pulled it closer to my hand.

"You been working here for a long time?" I asked.

She looked at me with her shy eyes and nodded.

"And is it really empty all the time, or is tonight an exception?"

I tried to sound serious because I really wanted to know. I hadn't been to this bar before. I already knew I didn't want to come back.

The brunette just shrugged her shoulders in answer. She placed the second glass of Jack on the bar.

I thought it was the right time to pay her. I took a fifty-dollar bill out of my wallet.

It was the only one in there, but she didn't know that. I laid it on the bar with a confident hand.

"Keep it," I said.

CHAPTER FIVE

The girl just took the money and put it under the desk without saying a single word. She leaned against the wooden shelf behind her and crossed her arms.

I turned around and said, "Well, perhaps this is also the 'place where nobody talks.'"

The old guy next to me slightly turned his head. As the overhead lamp lit the right half of his face, I saw that his skin was dry and rough like sandpaper.

His cheeks were hollow, like he was sucking them in. His forehead was furrowed with long, deep wrinkles.

Above his lips, an unkempt ginger mustache was hanging like a piece of wool. It looked dirty and needed a trim.

The little remaining hair on his skull was gathered in a greasy ponytail, sliding down to his back.

"Stacy can't talk, buddy," he said in a hoarse voice.

"Oh! Oh... I'm sorry!" I said to the girl. "Really! If I only knew... I'm sorry!"

She nodded and spread her lips in a humble smile.

"What about you?" I asked the man after a while. "Don't you like talking to somebody while you're drinking?"

He looked at me and sighed, "Whatcha want, buddy?"

"Nothing... I just...forget it!"

I turned around, took my drink, and moved a couple of chairs away from the guy. I didn't like talking to strangers.

I wasn't good company, either. And the closer I got to my forties, the harder it was for me to have a normal conversation with anybody.

CHAPTER SIX

I was sitting there, drinking fancy whiskey and pleasantly puffing gray smoke into the air. The warm alcohol was making me more and more relaxed.

The whiskey left a sweet aftertaste in my mouth. Besides that, I had new money. New success. It stood in my mind like a giant gate, ready to open.

All in all, it was a pleasant feeling.

The old fella searched his pockets, obviously looking for something. The search lasted less than a minute. He looked desperate. Like he couldn't find what he was looking for.

"Dammit!" the man swore, then said something to the guy sitting next to him.

He shook his finger in the air and pointed it towards his neck.

The man swore again, then glanced at me and cried out, "Hey!"

I pretended I wasn't hearing him.

"Hey, you there..."

I raised my eyebrow with a question on my face.

"You got a cigarette or two?"

This sounded like an invitation to me. I took my pack of Camels and my drink and sat next to the man.

CHAPTER SEVEN

He opened up the pack and pulled a cigarette out with his bony fingers. The knuckles of his hand were as bulged as bullets, swollen and hard.

"I'm Ezra," he mumbled and reached out his hand.

"Frank," I said. As I grabbed the guy's hand, I felt how rough and firm it was.

"So, Frank, lemme guess... lawyer?" Ezra asked.

I chuckled. "Far from the truth. I'm a writer."

"A writer? And what exactly do you write about, Frank?"

"I write about this and that..."

"This and that..." Ezra repeated and lit the cigarette up.

"Now's my turn. A truck driver?" I asked Ezra.

Ezra blew the smoke through his nose. "It's not so hard to guess."

"Do you have a family? Wife? Kids?"

"No," he said dryly.

"Have you been married?"

"Once. We divorced thirty years ago."

"Maybe it was for good," I said.

"Yeah, maybe."

"Have you ever wanted to get married again?"

"No."

"What, you don't like women anymore?" I joked. But a second later I realized it was a bad idea.

Ezra slowly turned to me. The light from the lamp lit up his entire face now.

I realized with a shock I hadn't really been able to see him before.

CHAPTER EIGHT

A pirate bandage crossed the left half of his face.
A round piece of leather covered his eye.

"Jesus Christ!" I pulled back.

"You see that?" Ezra pointed towards his left
eye. He leaned closer to me and said, "If you were
a woman, you wouldn't want me to be your man,
right? Not your friend, neighbor, lover—not even the
man sitting next to you while you're waiting for the
doctor."

Then he drew his face back and sipped from his
drink.

When I plucked up enough courage, I asked,
"How did that happen?"

"The Henry Woman," Ezra replied in an even
tone.

I gave him a puzzled look and asked, "Who's Henry and what the hell have you done to his wife to end up like that?"

Ezra looked at me and said, "You never heard about the Henry Woman?"

"No," I answered. "I think the only Henry I knew died last summer from a heart attack."

"So you've never heard the story about Sir Henry and Lady Annabelle?" Ezra asked, surprised.

By my confused look, Ezra already knew my answer to his question.

He took a couple of drags, then left the cigarette in the ashtray.

"Listen, buddy, I'm gonna tell you a story. I didn't believe it was true until *this* happened to me."

Ezra moved the bandage away.

The skin around his eye, his eyebrow, and cheekbone were scarred as if his face had been severely burned. His eyelid was closed, sunken deeply in his skull.

CHAPTER NINE

"The story says that at the end of the 19th century, a man called Henry—I can't remember his last name—lived in a nearby village. Everybody called him Sir Henry because he was considered to be an honorable and honest man.

"He was quite wealthy as well. He was a doctor. The people loved him. He never refused to help anybody.

"His wife's name was Annabelle. The people called her Lady Annabelle because of her husband's reputation for being so honest and honorable.

"Henry and Annabelle had three children—twin boys and a girl. They lived in a big house in the center of the village.

"One Sunday, Lady Annabelle went out to the local market. When she got home, she found a horrible and devastating scene.

"Sir Henry and the children had been slaughtered. Murdered like they weren't even human.

"Their throats were sliced. Their bodies were lying like dead pigs all over the ground. Everything was covered in blood and torn flesh.

"The only reason Lady Annabelle survived was because she wasn't in the house at that time.

"Nobody could figure out who did that terrible thing. It didn't seem like a robbery.

"A couple of weeks later, Lady Annabelle jumped off the bridge and drowned in the river. People say that she couldn't make it through after the shock.

"When they went to the morgue to take her body and to put it into the ground, they found nothing.

"Lady Annabelle was gone! At least her corpse was. Disappeared! Just like that!" Ezra said slowly and snapped his fingers.

CHAPTER TEN

Ezra told the story with a sort of cautiousness, even fear, I think.

His right eye was open the whole time, staring into his glass. It was like he was watching the scenes as he was telling them.

His face was calm and straight. But even though it was pretty dark in that bar, I could see Ezra had gone pale.

"But... a year later, strange things began to happen. Horrible things!" Ezra moaned.

"The people say the ghost of Lady Annabelle came back to the village and the nearby cities," Ezra said, circling his finger in the air. "She came to seek revenge! The Henry Woman—that's what they called her.

"They say that the Henry Woman uses the bodies of the living to do her deeds. Like some sort of intermediaries, you know. Puppets.

"I've heard different stories. A nurse who mutilated a patient. A nun who put out a boy's eyes. A hooker who sliced her client's genitals...

"One thing's always the same: the eyes! They go as black as tar, and just a single look and you go either blind, dumb, crippled, or deaf for the rest of your life."

"And why is that? I mean, why would she do this?"

"Revenge. Anger. Desperation. I don't know."

"And why are her victims always male?"

"Ask her, not me..."

"So you... met the Henry Woman?"

"Oh, yes! It happened on December 12, 1969—thirty years ago."

CHAPTER ELEVEN

Ezra took a sip of his drink before continuing.
I thought it was probably a good idea and did the same.

"I will never forget that day," he finally went on. "It was a harsh winter, and I was driving my regular route. The road was like glass. I could barely handle the truck.

"She was walking on the left side of the road. When I saw her, I hit the brakes. I managed to stop a couple of yards from her.

"I yelled, and she turned around and came to me. I couldn't see her face well, but... Those eyes! Hellish eyes! A true demon in the dark!"

Ezra slowly shook his head.

"I asked her where she was going and offered her a lift. After all, it was dark and freezing outside. The bitch lifted up her head, stared at me, and hissed like a snake. It was horrible!

"It's like my eye was set on fire from the inside. A burning sensation—like someone poured acid into my eyeball...

"When I woke up after that, I was lying in a hospital bed with bandages around my head like a damn mummy. I heard someone say, 'The right is fine, but the left is lost.'

"I knew they were talking about me. Since then, I wear this." Ezra pointed to his bandage.

"Johnsey met her too. Right, Johnsey?" Ezra asked the man next to him. "The Henry Woman?

"She had almost cut his throat. Just a single look and—ghrrrr." Ezra slid his finger on his throat. "His vocal chords are gone."

I nodded and glanced at the other guy. I thought about who looked worse—Ezra or the other fella. I couldn't choose.

They were two men with prematurely aged faces and prematurely ended lives.

Like some withered and broken version of Clint Eastwood and John Wayne, the old movie star.

They were doing nothing but drinking and thinking about their pasts and that weird woman.

CHAPTER TWELVE

"So what happened after that? Is that why your wife left you?" I asked Ezra.

"Oh, definitely! She never believed in what I told her. She left me three months later. I was a pretty ugly picture back then."

And you are now, too, I was tempted to say, but I kept the words in my head.

Listening to Ezra was getting a bit boring to me. I had never been able to sit in a chair for more than forty minutes.

And I couldn't listen to somebody's story for more than that either.

Plus, my eyes were getting heavy. The whiskey was making me feel sleepy. The thought of leaving the bar and going home seemed like a good one.

"I suggest you get one of these," Ezra said as he pulled something out of his chest pocket. "A wooden cross—the only way to protect yourself from the Henry Woman.

"I know a story about a guy who met her twice. The first time, he was nineteen. The second time, he was thirty-one.

"The first time, he lost his right arm. The second time, she came for the left. I don't wanna say 'good-bye' to my right eye, you know..."

I swallowed the last drop of whiskey and said, "Thanks, Ezra! I will think about that, but now I have to go. It's getting late. I don't want to meet your woman somewhere in the streets." I smiled.

"Sure. Take care, buddy! She can find you in the mornings, too, so beware!" Ezra warned me.

His warning was even boring. I just wanted to go home.

CHAPTER THIRTEEN

Outside the bar, the cold instantly woke me up. My lungs filled with fresh air. My body was shivering. My ears were echoing. My clothes smelled of cigarettes.

But I was out of the pit called Ronnie's. That was enough.

I was a couple of feet away from my car when put my hand in my pocket. The keys weren't there.

The picture of them on the bar next to the ashtray flashed in my mind. I turned around and headed toward the bar for the second time that evening.

But then, under the streetlights, I saw the girl with the brown hair coming toward me.

Something silvery was swaying in her hand. The

dim, yellow light from the bar reflected off it.

Surely it was my keys. I smiled, surprised by her act of kindness.

"You can't imagine how thankful I am!" I said in a pleasant tone.

She didn't reply. Instead, she reached her hand towards me. I took the keys.

I turned around to unlock the car and felt a chill creep up my back.

I saw the reflection of the girl in the car's window. The last thing I wanted to do was turn around

But I did it anyway.

CHAPTER FOURTEEN

Her eyes were dark black.

Her skin was as gray as a dead man. Her mouth opened wide like the jaws of a thirsty vampire. Her scream pierced my ears like hundreds of tiny needles.

I felt a burning, sharp pain in my left arm, just beneath the shoulder. It was like someone had wound a barbed wire around my bicep and had pulled with a single, sudden jerk.

The pain was so horrible. I immediately bent over and pressed my arm towards my chest. I coughed a few times, choked by the tightening sensation in my throat.

Then the girl slowly stepped back, turned

around, and headed to the bar.

I managed to get into the car, holding my arm next to my body. It was somehow numb and burning at the same time.

I had to find some help and I had to do it fast. It was the only way to save my arm and probably my life.

I got to St. Patrick Hospital and went into the emergency room. My hand was hanging like a piece of cloth fixed to my shoulder.

Some doctors quickly surrounded me, telling me to sit down and relax.

"The woman! The woman! The woman!" I was hysterical and shivering like a leaf.

"What woman, sir? Are there any more casualties?"

"The woman! The woman!"

"Calm down, sir! Tell us what happened!" one of the doctors said, moving my hand from around my bicep.

A nurse took my jacket off.

The doctors went silent and looked at my arm, horrified.

Its skin was ink black. It looked as if the flesh was dead or poisoned.

The black had spread all over my arm.

CHAPTER FIFTEEN

I must have fainted because I can't remember anything after that.

But here I am today. I'm sitting in my office, in
front of my typewriter, telling you the story about the
Henry Woman. And my encounter with her.

There's a wooden cross hanging on my neck.
I haven't taken it off for the last twelve months.

I sold the Toyota and bought a '99 Ford Escort
with an automatic transmission and diesel engine.

I'm typing with one hand—the right one.

My left hand was amputated. I think that it was
done by the Henry Woman, not really by some surgeon from St. Patrick's.

If you take a closer look at the photos before

the surgery, you can see a straight line going across my bicep. The tissue below that line is swollen and as dark as a coal.

The doctors had no explanation about the condition. I told them that I remembered nothing about what had happened to me. They didn't bother to ask anything else.

They called some man—a retired surgeon, I guess—to help them with the case.

The man said that he had seen three more cases like mine during his entire career. One of them was with a man called Frank Becks.

My grandfather's name was Frank Becks. His leg was amputated. I remember him wearing a wooden cross. I loved to play with it when I was a child.

Once, I asked him what happened to his leg.

He placed his finger on my lips and whispered, "Shhh! She's somewhere around, kid! She's somewhere around..."

About the Authors

Dylan Schatell, Emma Chambers, and Dinko Dinev are contributing authors to the Storyshares library.

About the Publisher

Storyshares is a publisher focused on supporting the millions of teens and adults who struggle with reading by creating a new shelf in the library specifically for them. The ever-growing collection features content that is compelling and culturally relevant for teens and adults, yet still readable at a range of lower reading levels.

Storyshares generates content by engaging deeply with writers, bringing together a community to create this new kind of book. With more intriguing and approachable stories to choose from, the teens and adults who have fallen behind are improving their skills and beginning to discover the joy of reading.

For more information, visit storyshares.org.

Easy to Read. Hard to Put Down.